STONE ARCH BOOKS
a capstone imprint

STONE ARCH BOOKS™
Published in 2012
A Capstone Imprint
1710 Roe Crest Drive
North Mankato, MN 56003
www.capstonepub.com

Originally published by DC Comics in the U.S. in single magazine form as Batman: The Brave and the Bold #1.

DC Comics
1700 Broadway, New York, NY 10019
A Warner Bros. Entertainment Company

Cataloging-in-Publication Data is available at the Library of Congress website:
ISBN: 978-1-4342-4545-8 (library binding)

Summary: A composite monster, controlled by the evil Lex Luthor, is on the rampage in England. Batman and Power Girl team up to stop it!

STONE ARCH BOOKS
Ashley C. Andersen Zantop *Publisher*
Michael Dahl *Editorial Director*
Donald Lemke & Christianne Jones *Editors*
Heather Kindseth *Creative Director*
Hilary Wacholz *Designer*
Kathy McColley *Production Specialist*

DC COMICS
Rachel Gluckstern & Michael Siglain *Original U.S. Editors*
Harvey Richards *U.S. Assistant Editor*
James Tucker *Cover Artist*

Printed in the United States of America in Brainerd, Minnesota.
122012 007078R

BATMAN
THE BRAVE AND THE BOLD®

MATT WAYNE....................WRITER
ANDY SURIANO....................PENCILLER
DAN DAVIS....................INKER
HEROIC AGE....................COLORIST
RANDY GENTILE....................LETTERER
JAMES TUCKER....................COVER ARTIST

HA! THERE'S NO ESCAPE, BATMAN! ONCE YOU'RE OUT OF THE WAY, ATLANTIS WILL BE MINE!
NOT SO FAST, CARAPAX... YOU'VE BEEN OUTMANEUVERED!
WHAT?
EVERY CRIMINAL MAKES ONE MISTAKE.
SHHBBBH
OOF!

YOU LET ME POSITION YOU BETWEEN A CORAL REEF AND AQUAMAN.
GOOD WORK, NELLYBELLE!
SOON...
BATMAN, OLD BEAN! THANKS TO YOU, WE CAN WRITE FINIS TO "THE STORY OF THE ROBOT THAT ATTACKED ME."
MAKE SURE YOU WIPE HIS COMPUTER MEMORY. THEN CARAPAX CAN BE SAFELY BROKEN DOWN AND STORED IN YOUR ROYAL ATLANTEAN VAULT.
BEEEP
YES, OF COURSE... WHAT SAY WE SCARE UP SOME HERRING FOR LUNCH? DID I EVER TELL YOU ABOUT THE TIME I WRESTLED A PREHISTORIC OCTOPUS?
I CALL IT "THE TALE OF THAT TIME I WRESTLED THAT PREHISTORIC OCTOPUS...."
EXCUSE ME. I HAVE TO TAKE THIS.
IT'S ALFRED, SIR. YOUR BUTLER? YOU DO REMEMBER THAT YOU HAVE A HOME, SIR?
GO AHEAD.
YOU'VE RECEIVED A DISTRESS CALL FROM LONDON ON THE SECURE LINE...

I WOULDN'T HAVE DISTURBED YOU, SIR, BUT THE PRIME MINISTER DID SAY IT WAS RATHER URGENT.
RAARRRGH
UNDERGROUND

UBB
ALFRED ISN'T KIDDING. WHAT IS THAT THING, AND HOW DID IT GET HERE?
KRUMP
AND HOW DO I STOP IT?
FOOMP
THESE PRISM PELLETS WILL DISORIENT THE CREATURE...
POONT
...AND BUY ME TIME TO BREAK OUT THE SLEEPING GAS.

KLATTER
HUFFF
KRASSH
RARRGGH!!
INCREDIBLE! ENOUGH GAS TO KNOCK OUT A HUNDRED PEOPLE, AND IT ONLY MADE THE MONSTER ANGRY!
NEARBY...
IGNORE THAT BAT-PIPSQUEAK! GO, MY COMPOSITE CREATURE! GO TO THE TOWER OF LONDON! HA! HA!
GRAB THE CROWN JEWELS OF THE UNITED KINGDOM AND RETURN TO ME! GO! GO! GO!

ACE PROGRAMMER KAREN STARR ADDRESSES A SOFTWARE CONFERENCE ONE BLOCK AWAY...
WITH THE SAME 5-D TELEMETRIC ALGORITHM SET, WE CAN SEE INSIDE THE ELECTRON, OR DETECT INSTABILITIES IN THE EARTH'S CORE.
OR EVEN MAKE A CUTTING-EDGE GAME PLATFORM. THANK--
--YOUOOF!
WHAT WAS THAT?
EARTHQUAKE!
KA-THOOM
EARTHQUAKES IN LONDON? SINCE WHEN? I'D BETTER INVESTIGATE--NOT AS KAREN STARR, OF COURSE...
...BUT AS POWER GIRL

POOMT
THIS THING WON'T EVEN SLOW DOWN! NO MATTER WHAT, IT KEEPS HEADING TOWARD THE *TOWER OF LONDON!*
HAVE TO FIND A WAY TO STOP IT!
WOOOOSH!
RENNCH
UH-OH.
ALFRED! CALL THE QUEEN AND TELL HER TO EXECUTE *PLAN 778.*
POOMT

SHWIPP
CRIPES, BATS! IF YOU TRY TO TIE THIS THING DOWN, WE'LL BE HERE ALL DAY!
POWER GIRL?
LEMME JUST HANG A COUPLE GOOD ONES ON MONSTER-BOY'S CHIN...
WOULD YOU MIND NOT PUNCHING ME IN THE FACE? I'M ALREADY IN A BIT OF A SPOT, DON'T YOU KNOW.

I SAY.
RAW-THER.
THIS CREATURE'S MADE OUT OF INNOCENT ENGLISH PEOPLE. HUNDREDS OF THEM! I CAN'T HIT THE CREATURE WITHOUT INJURING THEM.
POWER GIRL!
HELP ME TIE IT DOWN!

SHORTLY...
RARRRGH!
HOPE THE TOWER BRIDGE WON'T MISS A FEW CABLES!
THEY WON'T HOLD FOR LONG. BUT MAYBE LONG ENOUGH TO SAVE THESE POOR SOULS. WHOEVER DID THIS TO THEM MUST STILL BE NEARBY.
I DUNNO, SCANNING THE WHOLE CITY WITH MY X-RAY VISION COULD TAKE HOURS...
A FEW MILES BACK, I SAW A BOARDED-UP BUILDING WITH A GOOD VIEW OF THE TOWER.
BINGO! THAT EVIL SCIENTIST, LUTHOR, HAS SET UP INSIDE!
I MIGHT HAVE KNOWN. HERE'S THE PLAN...
POWER GIRL! WAIT!
SHWOOOM

UNDO WHATEVER YOU DID TO THOSE POOR ENGLISH PEOPLE!
POWER GIRL, TOO, EH?
FREE YOURSELF, CREATURE! FIND THE JEWELS! HURRY!
WHAT WAS THAT? DO YOU REALLY WANT TO PLAY GAMES WITH ME, LUTHOR?
HO-HUM. ANOTHER MOUTHY, BULLETPROOF OAF, OUT TO SPOIL MY CRIME.
W-WHY ARE YOU GETTING SO HEAVY?
SIMPLETON. YOU'RE STANDING IN THE RAYS OF MY RED SUN LAMP!
I'D BEEN DEVELOPING IT TO USE ON THAT OTHER KRYPTONIAN BUSYBODY, SUPERMAN!
KLK

TRY AND STOP ME NOW, POWERLESS GIRL!
NO POWERS?
NOW YOU'RE ANOTHER DOLT IN A COSTUME! YOU'RE NOTHING! A WEAK, INSIGNIFICANT HUMAN!
I'M STILL IN BETTER SHAPE THAN YOU!
POW
FZZT
SERIOUSLY, LUTHOR, PASS UP A DONUT ONCE IN A WHILE.
GROAN

NOW LET'S SEE... WHOOPS! GOT AROUND YOUR ENCRYPTION FAST ENOUGH... WHAT'S THIS?
TAPPITA-TAPPITA-TAP-TAP-TAP
A FOLDER MARKED "CONCATENATION RAY," AND A PASSWORD PROMPT! HMM... DON'T SUPPOSE YOU'D JUST TELL ME THE PASSWORD, HUH?
LUTHOR?
W-WHAT KIND OF GUN IS THAT?
IT'S A TELEPORTATION RAY THAT DOESN'T QUITE WORK YET.
BACK AWAY FROM THE KEYBOARD, PLEASE. THIS WILL BE MESSY.
IN THAT CASE...
...EAT IT OVER THE SINK!
WHUDD

BATMAN, AM I EVER GLAD TO SEE YOU!
MAYBE NEXT TIME, YOU WON'T RUN OFF WITHOUT A PLAN.

HASTE MAKES WASTE. IN CRIMEBUSTING, EVEN MORE WASTE THAN USUAL.

SO, LUTHOR. YOU'RE THE SICK GENIUS BEHIND THIS... CROWD MONSTER.
COMPOSITE CREATURE, BATMAN!

ONE BLAST OF MY CONCATENATION RAY LET ME SHAPE EVERY HUMAN WITHIN SIX CITY BLOCKS INTO THE FORM OF MY CHOOSING!
SOON, IT WILL BREAK YOUR PATHETIC BONDS, COMPLETE ITS TASK, AND RETURN TO ME! AND THEN I'LL HAVE IT DEAL WITH YOU!

THE CROWN JEWELS AREN'T THERE, LUTHOR.
WHEN I SAW THE MONSTER HEAD TOWARD THE TOWER, I ALERTED THE AUTHORITIES. THE YEOMAN WARDERS RAN THEM OUT THE BACK DOOR BEFORE YOUR MONSTER EVER ATTACKED.
IDIOT! THE CREATURE WILL DESTROY THE CITY LOOKING FOR THOSE JEWELS!
YOUR INTERFERENCE HAS DOOMED THE HUNDREDS INSIDE MY CREATURE, AND THOUSANDS MORE ONCE IT BREAKS LOOSE! HA! HA!
THE PASSWORD IS WHAT...?
GUESS.

LET'S SEE... RANDOM LETTERS AND NUMBERS ARE ALWAYS THE SAFEST CHOICE. BUT INSTEAD, MOST PEOPLE CHOOSE SOMETHING IMPOSSIBLE TO FORGET.
SUCH AS THE NAME OF A RELATIVE, OR A FRIEND, OR EVEN AN ENEMY.
SUPERMAN.
NOW WHO'S THE DOLT, LUTHOR?
TAPPITA-TAP
BIDDIP
UP-DOWN-UP-UP-UP-DOWN-UP. ACCORDING TO THESE SCHEMATICS, THAT SEQUENCE SHOULD REVERSE THE CONCATENATION CIRCUIT.
ZZZZSHRAKKKKT

RARRRGH
SHLOBBB

GLOOOOOP
STRIKE A LIGHT, GUV! IT'S AS IF 'UNDREDS OF US WAS COMBINED INTO A MONSTER!
RUBBISH! CLEARLY SOME SORT OF MASS HALLUCINATION, WOT?
JOLLY GOOD SHOW, BATMAN!

SO... WHERE DID THE JEWELS END UP, ANYWAY?
BATMAN! THANK YOU EVER SO MUCH! AS SOON AS WE GOT YOUR MESSAGE, WE STASHED THE LOOT IN BUCKINGHAM PALACE.
THAT IS THE WORD? "LOOT"?
THAT'S CORRECT YOUR HIGHNESS!
SOON...
AWW, A MEDAL... SHE'S SUCH A SWEETIE!
YOU DESERVE IT. FOR ALL YOUR STRENGTH, IT WAS THE BRUTE FORCE OF YOUR CHARACTER THAT SAVED ALL THESE PEOPLE.
MEH, WE'D NEVER LET INNOCENT BYSTANDERS GET HURT. LUTHOR WAS COUNTING ON THAT.
TRUE, BUT CRIMINALS ALWAYS MAKE ONE MISTAKE...HE NEVER COUNTED ON BEING OUTWITTED.
WELL, THIS BRAINY HERO CAN'T WAIT TO START PUNCHING THROUGH CONCRETE AGAIN...
...BUT FIRST I'LL HAVE TO SOAK UP SOME SUNLIGHT.
THEN BY ALL MEANS, POWER GIRL, LET'S GET YOU OUT OF FOGGY LONDON!
END.

LEX LUTHOR

Lex Luthor is a criminal mastermind of Metropolis, as brilliant as he is ruthless. He uses his gifts to plan stunning crimes that he thinks prove his superiority. This super-villain won't rest until he is rich and his enemies are destroyed.

TOP SECRET:

Born into extreme poverty, Lex Luthor was tempted early by the easy money to be had in a life of evil.

POWER GIRL

A survivor of the destruction of planet Krypton in a parallel universe, Power Girl has the same amazing Kryptonian abilities as Superman.

TOP SECRET:

In her secret identity as programmer Karen Starr, Power Girl is dedicated to developing software that can predict if Earth will ever become geologically unstable, like her shattered homeworld.

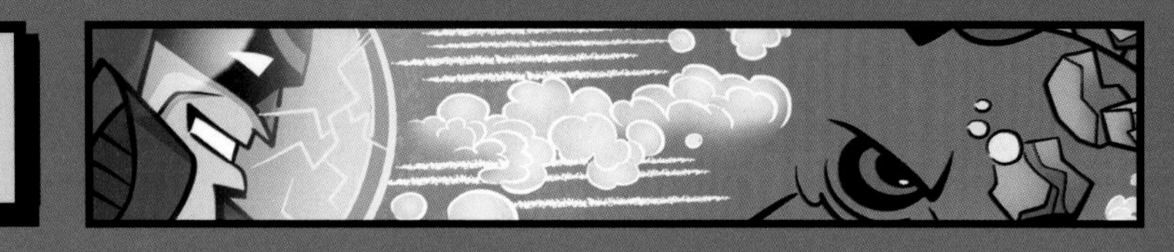

MATT WAYNE WRITER

Matt Wayne is a writer who has worked on TV series including *Ben 10: Ultimate Alien*, *Static Shock*, *Danny Phantom,* and the animated movie *Hellboy: Storm of Swords*. He was an editor at Milestone Media, and has written comics including *Hardware*, *Shadow Cabinet*, *Justice League Unlimited*, and more.

ANDY SURIANO PENCILLER

Andy Suriano is an illustrator of both comic books and animation. His comic book credits include *Batman: The Brave and the Bold* and *Doc Bizarre, M.D.* He's worked on popular animated television series as well, such as *Samurai Jack* and *Star Wars: The Clone Wars.*

DAN DAVIS INKER

Dan Davis is a comic illustrator for DC Comics, Warner Bros., and Bongo. His work has been nominated for several Eisner Awards, including his work on *Batman: The Brave and the Bold*. During his career, Davis has illustrated Batman, The Simpsons, Harry Potter, Samurai Jack, and many other well-known characters!

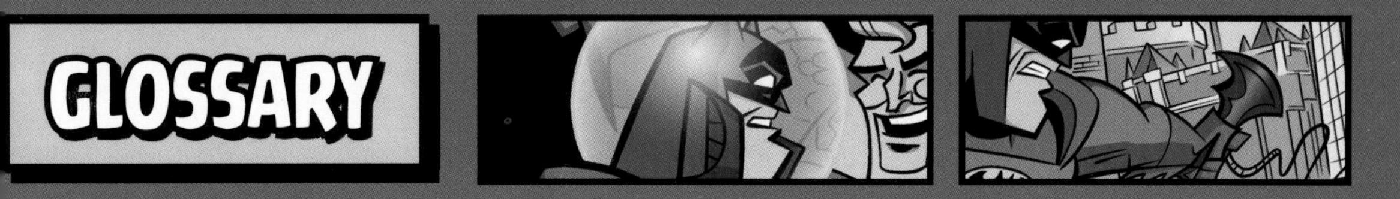

composite [kuhm-POZ-it] - made up of various parts or elements

disorient [diss-OR-ee-uhnt] - to cause confusion

distress [diss-TRESS] - a feeling of great pain or sadness

haste [HAYST] - speed or quickness in moving or acting

insignificant [in-sig-NIF-uh-kuhnt] - not important

outmaneuvered [out-muh-NOO-verd] - to overcome an opponent by using clever maneuvers or skills

prehistoric [pree-hi-STOR-ik] - belonging to a time before history was recorded in written form

schematics [ske-MAT-iks] - a diagram, especially of an electrical or mechanical system

VISUAL QUESTIONS & PROMPTS

1. This Batman adventure is titled *The Panic of the Composite Creature*. At which panel did you realize what the Composite Creature was made out of? Did you feel like there were enough clues in the story to figure it out, or would you have named the book something else?

2. Most of this story takes place in London, England. Look at the panel at right and name at least two elements that help show that the story takes place in London.

3. When Power Girl starts fighting Luthor on page 15, the panels turn red. This color change in the panels tells you something is happening. What?

4. A character's expression can tell you a lot about how he or she is feeling. Study the image at right. How do you think Batman is feeling? Use the image to explain your answer.

5. A person's expressions, poses, or gestures can sometimes show whether they are good or evil. Could you tell that Luthor was evil without reading the text? Explain your answer.

READ THEM ALL!

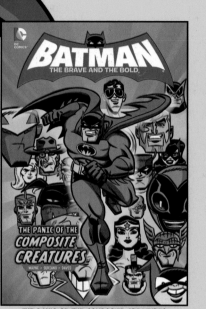